Big Mouth ELIZABETH

Big Mouth ELIZABETH

An A Is for Elizabeth Book

written by
Rachel Vail

illustrated by
Paige Keiser

Feiwel and Friends
New York

A FEIWEL AND FRIENDS BOOK
An imprint of Macmillan Publishing Group, LLC
175 Fifth Avenue, New York, NY 10010

Our books may be purchased in bulk for promotional,
educational, or business use. Please contact your local
bookseller or the Macmillan Corporate and Premium Sales
Department at (800) 221-7945 ext. 5442 or by email
at MacmillanSpecialMarkets@macmillan.com.

Library of Congress Cataloging-in-Publication Data
Names: Vail, Rachel, author. | Keiser, Paige, illustrator.
Title: Big mouth Elizabeth / by Rachel Vail ;
illustrated by Paige Keiser.
Description: First edition. | New York : Feiwel and Friends,
[2019] | Summary: Elizabeth, the younger sister of Justin Case,
is frustrated about being one of the few Class 2B students
to still have all of her baby teeth.
Identifiers: LCCN 2018039305 | ISBN 9781250162175 (hardcover) |
ISBN 9781250162182 (ebook)
Subjects: | CYAC: Schools—Fiction. | Teeth—Fiction. |
Growth—Fiction. | Clubs—Fiction.
Classification: LCC PZ7.V1916 Big 2019 | DDC [E]—dc23
LC record available at https://lccn.loc.gov/2018039305

Book design by Liz Dresner
Feiwel and Friends logo designed by Filomena Tuosto

First edition, 2019
1 3 5 7 9 10 8 6 4 2
mackids.com

To my friend Meg,
with love and prizes —R. V.

For Aunt Betty —P. K.

Chapter 1

In Class 2B, we are all friends.

We are friends with everybody in the whole class.

It is not easy.

My challenge is Anna.

Also Smelly Dan.

And Babyish Cali.

But mostly Anna.

Chapter 2

This morning, Anna brought a huge, fat book from home for morning reading time.

Anna is a show-off.

Then she whispered to my best friend, Bucky, during lineup to go out to recess.

I made angry eyes at Anna's back
the whole way outside.

She got on the good swing, because
she always does.

I am a fast runner, too, so I got to
the second-best swing.

I pretended I was flying.

I was being Super Elizabeth, who
can fly higher than Ordinary Anna.

I smiled at her, to be nice.

Superheroes who can fly highest
are also polite.

She smiled back.

It was a scary smile.

"WHY IS YOUR MOUTH
BLEEDING?" I asked Anna.

We both dragged our feet to slow
down.

Chapter
3

We got off the swings.

I looked in Anna's open mouth.

Her fingers reached in and came out holding a popcorn, I thought.

"Ooooh! Elizabeth punched Anna!" Smelly Dan yelled, jumping off the slide. "Oooh!"

"No, she didn't!" Bucky said.

"Ewww," Babyish Cali shrieked. "She's bleeding!"

"Why did you punch Anna?" Zora asked me.

"I didn't!" I yelled.

"What happened?" Mallory asked, all calm like a teacher.

Smelly Dan shouted, "Oooooh! I'm

telling! Elizabeth punched Anna in the mouth!"

"I did not," I told him. "Pipe down, you."

This is what I mean about Smelly Dan.

He is always trying to make trouble.

Chapter
4

Anna held up the little popcorn-looking thing. "It's my tooth," she said.

"Ewww!" Babyish Cali screamed.

This is what I mean about Babyish Cali.

She is always being babyish.

"It's not your first lost tooth, is it,
Anna?" Mallory asked.

"No," Anna said. "My second.
Ugh."

She spat.

A glob of blood landed on the mat.

"EWWWW!" Babyish Cali screeched.
"I'm scared of blood!"

She turned around and sat down.

Chapter 5

Mr. Cortez, the teacher of 2A, was walking toward us to see what was going on.

Before he got to us, Mallory took charge.

"You can choose who you want to walk you to the nurse," Mallory told Anna.

Anna looked at each face.
I smiled very nicely.
Anna is annoying.
But it is always a good feeling to be chosen.

Chapter
6

Anna chose Mallory.

Well, I don't like the nurse's office anyway.

Or blood.

I'm not scared of it.

I just don't love it.

Mallory put her arm around Anna's shoulders as they walked in.

If I get chosen to walk someone with a lost tooth and bleeding mouth to the nurse someday, I will do that.

If I lose a tooth someday, maybe I will choose Mallory.

Mallory is good at walking a person to the nurse.

Chapter
7

Anna is not Mallory's best friend.
Rose is.

Rose watched Mallory go into the
school with her arm around Anna.

Rose is in 2A this year.

She's not in 2B like me and Anna
and Mallory.

You probably can't be best friends
with someone in the other class.
So maybe Mallory has an opening.

Chapter
8

Anna got a special little box with gold squiggles from the nurse.

Inside the box, the slightly disgusting tiny tooth rested on a fluffy cotton cloud.

Everybody got to look, but just for three seconds: 3-2-1.

No touching.

Anna was the star of class 2B.

As usual.

"How many teeth have you lost, Elizabeth?" Mallory asked me after I passed Anna's tooth box to her.

"Zero," I said.

"Really?" Mallory asked. "Zero? You have all your baby teeth?"

"And you're in second grade?" Anna asked.

"Yes," I said. "See? Here I am."

"Weird," Mallory said.

Bucky smiled at me from his seat
next to Anna. He has no front teeth
at all.

I kept my lips closed over my baby
teeth. And sank low in my seat.

Bucky is my best friend, but
sometimes he does not help.

Chapter

9

I had a scary dream.

I don't remember most of it, but I do remember one thing.

It was: My teeth were all falling out.

It was scary.

When I woke up, I ran right to the bathroom and checked in the mirror.

All the baby teeth were still in.

I was happy.

Then I was sad.

Then I had an idea!

I loaded up lots of toothpaste and brushed sooooo much.

I was hoping to loosen some of those baby teeth up.

Sometimes Dad says, "Do a good job brushing your teeth, Elizabeth!"

Not today.

This morning he yelled,
"Elizabeth, enough!"
I don't know
how you tell
when it's enough.

Chapter 10

When I got onto the bus going to
school, Bucky moved over.

I sit with him every day.

We are all friends in Class 2B.

We don't have best friends.

But Bucky is mine.

I sat down next to him.

He smiled at me.

I did not smile back.

He was showing off his lack of teeth.

Showing off is not nice.

"You are a grump," Bucky said.

"You are a show-off," I said.

"Want some pretzels?" Bucky asked.

We shared his pretzels.

At snack, I will share my apple slices so he won't have just the empty pretzel bag.

He is a show-off of lost teeth, but he is still my best friend.

Chapter
11

Ms. Patel said *good morning* to each of us as we walked into class.

She smiled at me when she was saying "Good morning, Elizabeth."

She has nice teeth.

All big ones.

Why are my teeth so little? I was thinking, slumped in my chair.

Mallory was whispering to Anna.

Anna smiled her big lost-tooth smile the whole morning.

I sit behind her, but I could tell she was show-off smiling from the back of her head.

Chapter

12

At recess, there was a meeting of a new club.

The name of the club is THE BIG MOUTH CLUB.

It is a club of girls who have lost baby teeth and started getting big teeth.

"Sorry," Mallory said to me. She tipped her head to the side, like she was being nice.

Mallory's best friend, Rose, put her hands on her hips and looked at my mouth. "Why do you still have all your baby teeth, anyway?" Rose asked me.

I didn't answer because:

1. I don't know why I still have all my baby teeth, anyway.
2. If you have nothing nice to say, you can stay quiet, Mom says.
3. I had only mean things to say to Rose about that question.

Mallory said, "Maybe you and Cali could make a Baby Mouth Club together."

I didn't say anything to that either because:

1. I didn't want to be in a Baby Mouth Club.
2. I didn't want to be in a club with Babyish Cali.
3. I didn't want to cry and seem like even more of a baby.

Chapter
13

My grandparents Gingy and Poopsie were babysitting me after school.

Grandparents are old, so they should have good ideas by now.

"I'm trying to lose some of my teeth," I explained to Gingy and Poopsie.

"I'm trying to keep all mine," Poopsie said.

"You don't have baby teeth," I said.

"Your teeth are perfect," Gingy said.

"They are BABY teeth and I'm not a BABY," I yelled. "In fact, you should be KID-sitting me!"

"She has a point," Poopsie said.

"Have a snack," Gingy said. "To go with that point."

I slumped at the table between Poopsie and my dog, Qwerty.

"Anything loose?" Poopsie whispered.

I checked. One bottom tooth seemed like a possibility.

Poopsie checked, too. "Not quite ripe," he said. "Keep wiggling it."

"Really?" I asked. "Mom said that doesn't work."

"What does she know?" Poopsie asked. "I'm her dad. To me, she's a baby."

I laughed.

"I know how to get a loose tooth out," Poopsie whispered.

"Really?" Qwerty and I weren't sure.

"It's easy! You get it loose, I'll get it out. Here comes Gingy. Shhh."

Chapter 14

When Mom and Dad came home, I
asked Mom if Poopsie really knows
how to make baby teeth fall out.

"When I was a kid and had a loose
tooth, Poopsie tied a string around it,"
Mom said.

"Why?" I asked.

"He tied the other end of the string to a doorknob and then slammed the door shut!"

"He did not," Gingy said.

"He did so!" Mom said. "That's how I lost that tooth!"

"He said he would, but he didn't," Gingy said. She winked at me. "He never did."

I closed my mouth over my baby teeth and looked at Poopsie.

He shrugged. "Maybe I did, maybe I didn't. Pass the Jell-O!"

Gingy shook her head but passed him the Jell-O she'd made.

Sometimes in my family it is hard to know who's telling the truth.

Chapter

15

"It's past bedtime, Elizabeth!" Mom said. "Why are you jumping around like a monkey?"

"I'm trying to shake some of my baby teeth loose," I explained.

"What's the rush to lose your

teeth?" Mom asked, sitting down on my bed.

I had to tell her the truth. "I'm one of the only kids in second grade with none lost yet."

"Everybody does things at a different pace," Mom said.

"I hate having a different pace from all my friends," I said.

"That is hard," Mom said. "Hang in there, pal."

"Yeah, well I'm trying to *hang in there, pal*," I said. "That's hard, too!"

"I know," Mom said.

"I don't like things that are hard." I flopped down next to her.

"Nobody does," Mom said, cuddling me up, "which is rough because not everything in life is easy."

"Like baby teeth that won't fall out."

"Yeah. That is hard," Mom said. "Sometimes I wish I could just wave a wand and make everything easy for you."

"Me too," I said. "Please do that."

"But even if I could, maybe I wouldn't," Mom said.

"WHAT," I said. "You should, Mom! You totally should. Do you have that wand?"

"No, nobody has one," Mom said. "But sometimes it's the hard stuff that makes life *interesting*."

"Not to me," I said.

"You make yourself stronger and braver when you face challenges,"

Mom said. "It's how you find out what you're made of!"

"I'm made of blood and skin and baby teeth," I said, very sad.

"I mean, you find out who you really are."

"I'm really Elizabeth," I reminded her.

"Oh, good," Mom said, kissing my forehead. "Because Elizabeth is a very brave kid, who is up way past bedtime. I love you. Good night, Elizabeth."

"Bad night, Mom," I said.

She patted my hair and left, turning out my light on her way.

Chapter 16

Even in the dark, I had all baby teeth and no magic wands.

Qwerty has big teeth, but he only speaks dog.

My dog-rabbit, Dolores, has no teeth at all, so she had no advice.

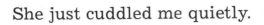

She just cuddled me quietly.

Chapter
17

Today we got put into reading groups.

At least I'm not in the Yellow Group with Babyish Cali.

I'm in the Blue Reading Group.

Mallory is in Blue also.

That is the good news.

Smelly Dan is also in Blue.

That is the second-to-worst news.

Here is the worst news:

My best friend, Bucky, is with
Anna and Zora and Silent Fiona in the
Purple Group.

We don't have a top group in 2B,
but everybody gets it anyway, what
the rankings are.

Chapter 18

I was a grump the whole afternoon.

I was still a grump when I got home from school.

Even though Mom was home and there were cookies.

Anna was in the top group in 1A, also, I explained to Mom.

Anna could read before kindergarten.

She didn't get in trouble for that. She got compliments.

Knowing how to read before kindergarten is against the rules, I think.

Mom said, "Well, no, I don't think that's actually a rule."

Bucky learned to read during kindergarten.

Last year in 1A, he was in the top group, too.

He sat next to Anna in first-grade reading circles.

Near the door.

Far away from me and my group of "can't read" babies.

Having a different pace from your best friend is very not easy.

It makes a person's heart hurt.

Chapter
19

I thought that was all the bad news
for today, but no.

Babyish Cali called me on the
phone tonight.

"It's for you," Mom said. "It's your
friend Cali."

I shook my head *no*.

"Come to the phone, Elizabeth."
Mom smiled at me like *I mean it*.

I shook my head like a tornado of
NO.

Mom stopped smiling and held the
phone at me. "Now, please."

I didn't want to but I had to.

"Hi," I said into the phone.

Babyish Cali asked, "Do you want
to come over on Saturday?"

I am not allowed to be rude or
to lie.

I had to think of an answer that
wouldn't be rude or a lie.

"I'll ask my mom," I said.

My mom was making a question
face at me.

"Great," Cali said. "Go ahead."

I took a big breath and looked at
Mom.

"Can I go to Cali's house Saturday?" I asked Mom, while shaking my head NO for DON'T LET ME.

But Mom nodded and shrugged like *sure, why not.*

So I didn't answer anything to Cali.

"I thought you might be free because of not being in the Big Mouth Club," Cali was saying.

"Why would that make me free on Saturday?" I asked.

"Because they're all going to Playland Saturday."

"Playland?"

I love Playland.

"It's a Big-Mouth-Club-only trip," Babyish Cali said.

"Oh," I said.

"You could come over to my house," Cali said.

"Okay," I said.

"Great!" said Babyish Cali.

"Great," I said, too.

But my *great* was a lie.

Chapter
20

Tonight for homework in the Blue
Group, we have to write something we
wish would happen.

I wish I would lose a tooth or
three so I could be in the Big Mouth
Club and get invited to Playland

with Mallory and Anna and Rose on
Saturday.

That is my true wish.

But what if Ms. Patel makes me
read it out loud?

Anna and Mallory might laugh at
me, with all their lack of baby teeth
showing.

Chapter
21

NAME: *El!zabeth!*

I WISH: *all the dogs at the rescue place could get adopted by families that will love them. Very much. Very, very much.*

And that everything would be easy.

The End

Thank you.
By El!zabeth!

Chapter
22

Good thing I didn't tell my true wish, because I was right: We had to read our homework out loud. Not to the whole class. But still, to the whole Blue Group.

Mallory's homework was so funny. Her younger brother, Mikey, is almost three, but he says it like "two and flee tawters."

She wrote that she wished Mikey would not touch her with his buttery hands every morning, and also that instead of a brother, she had a hamster.

But then, she wrote a PS.

A PS means it's at the end and you whisper it, like a secret.

Her PS said:

I just went in to look at Mikey. He was sleeping. I change my wish. I wish Mikey could just stay so cute and sweet forever. Even tho I know that wish won't come true.

Now I wish I had a buttery baby brother, too.

Mallory said she liked my wish about the dogs.

That only made me wish my real wish more, about the teeth and the club.

Even tho I know that wish won't come true.

Chapter
23

I thought of a good
challenge for myself!
Lose a tooth!
Tonight!
If I can manage to lose
a tooth tonight, I could
find out who I really am.

And who I am would be: *somebody who is in the Big Mouth Club.*

I have to ask if Gingy and Poopsie are coming over tonight.

Poopsie's string idea sounds terrible, but Mom says I am a brave kid, so maybe I can handle it.

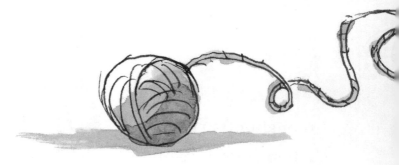

Chapter 24

Nope.

My not-buttery brother, Justin, has no baby teeth anymore.

But he is no help at all, either.

He said when his first tooth fell out, he threw up and lost his tooth down the drain.

I said, "I wish you were a hamster."

He whispered all mean, "Get out of my room."

Mom only heard what I said, not what Justin said.

So now me and all my baby teeth are sitting here alone in my room until I can be pleasant.

There is no way I can be pleasant.

So I might never get out of here.

I am going to start my homework for Monday.

I have to write a story where something that I wish actually happens.

All I have so far is the title:

"The Night My Brother, Justin, Turned into a Hamster."

Chapter 25

"Are you down
in the dumps
again?" Bucky
asked me at recess.
"Yes," I said.
"Why?" he asked.

"Because I am left out of the Big Mouth Club."

"I am, too," he said.

"It's only girls!"

"So I'm definitely not in it?"

"I guess not," I said.

"That's not fair!" he said.

"You're right!" I agreed. "It's not! Are you down in the dumps with me now?"

"No," he said.

"Why not?"

"I don't know," he said. "Nobody can be in every club."

"Yeah, but . . ." I said.

"Yeah, but . . ." he said. He laughed. "You said *Yeah but*."

I laughed, too. "Yeah, but."

"Let's run around," he said.

Chapter
26

So we did.

And that is why Bucky
is my best friend.

Still.

The Big Mouth Club is the club I most want to be in.

So all afternoon, even when Science Teacher Sal came with her cart?

I was back down in the dumps.

Chapter 28

Tonight, the phone rang.

Usually, it is Gingy calling.

"Elizabeth!" Dad yelled.

I ran down.

It wasn't Gingy.

It was Anna.

She had great news to tell me.

Chapter
29

"Great news," Anna said. "Rose has lice."

"Mice?" I asked.

"Lice," Anna said. "You know, little bugs in her hair."

"Ewww," I said. "How is hair bugs great news?"

"For you!" Anna said. "Rose can't go to Playland tomorrow!"

"Because of the lice?"

"Yes," said Anna. "So there is an extra seat in the car! You can be in the seat!"

"What about my teeth?"

"Do you have any loose ones?" she asked.

"Yes," I lied. "A bunch of loose ones."

"Great," Anna said. "Mallory said you can be a junior member of the club. Ask if you can go and call me back."

Chapter 30

Mom said, "Elizabeth, you already
have other plans tomorrow.
Remember?"

"But I would rather go to Playland
and be in the Big Mouth Club!" I
explained.

"Big Mouth Club?" Mom asked.

"It means you have grown-up teeth, Mom," I explained.

"Usually, it's an insult," Mom said. "If you call someone a big mouth."

"Why?"

"It means they, well, say things they shouldn't. Or they talk too much. It's mean. Is someone calling you a big mouth?"

"No!" I yelled. "They are NOT!"

"Well, good," Mom said. "I don't like name-calling."

"I love Playland! Please let me go!" I begged. "PLEASE!"

"No," Mom said. "You already have plans with another friend."

Chapter
31

Now I am back in my room to Think
About It.

WHAT I HAVE TO THINK ABOUT:

1. Why I should not throw myself
   on the floor screaming when I
   don't like Mom's decision.

2. How would Babyish Cali feel if I said, *Too bad on you! I am going to Playland!*

Chapter 32

WHAT I THINK ABOUT IT:

1. I should not throw myself on the floor screaming when I don't like Mom's decision, because all that happens is I have to go to my room. She doesn't even change her mind.

2. I am not Babyish Cali. I can't know how she would feel.

But here is how I *think* Babyish Cali would feel:

Down in the dumps.

Chapter 33

"Sorry, Anna," I said. "I already have plans for tomorrow with Cali, so I can't come."

"With Babyish Cali?" Anna asked.

"Yes," I said.

"Oh," said Anna.

I didn't know what to say to that.

"Well, have fun," Anna said, and hung up.

But it sounded like what she meant was:

There is no way that will be fun. Too bad on you.

I did not throw myself on the floor and scream.

I kept that inside.

Only an angry look at Mom was on my outside.

Chapter
34

Mom said a good way to have a good day is to decide it's a good day.

I said, "I am carsick."

I don't know how a person can just decide it is a good day when it is a bad day because she is in the car

on the way to Babyish Cali's house
instead of going to Playland with the
Big Mouth Club.

That sounds to me like *lying*.

Chapter
35

The moms decided to have a cup of tea on the patio.

Babyish Cali took me up the stairs to see her room.

Up and up and up.

Cali has a thousand stairs.

"Sometimes we go sledding on them," Babyish Cali said.

"How can you sled on stairs?" I
asked. "Does it snow inside your
house?"

"No," said Babyish Cali.

She opened the door to her room.

Chapter
36

Chapter
37

"This is the coolest room I ever saw," I said. "Who built all this?"

"I did," she said.

"Are these experiments?" I asked. "Or, like, inventions?"

"Some of each," she said in her squeaky voice.

She flipped a switch and a little train carried a rock around the top of her room.

"Press this," she said.

I did.

The rock dropped onto her bed.

"Wow!" I yelled. "You're amazing!"

Babyish Cali giggled. "You are so nice, Elizabeth."

Well, I am not sure if that's true.

"We can play anything you want," Babyish Cali said.

I looked around, thinking about it.

Everything looked like stuff I'm not old enough to play with.

"Or do you want to sled on the steps?" she asked.

"How?" I asked.

"Pillows!" she said.

Chapter
38

We stood at the top of Babyish Cali's stairs, holding our pillows.

I didn't want to be babyish.

More babyish than Babyish Cali.

But I was very scared.

"Is this allowed?" I asked.

"We do it all the time," Babyish Cali said.

Maybe she is not so babyish, I thought.

Maybe she is just short and cute.

And neat.

And naughty.

And brave.

Maybe Mom was wrong about me.

I sure didn't feel brave.

"You can go first," Cali said. "You're the guest."

"You're the host," I said.

I was hugging that pillow very much.

Chapter 39

Is it babyish to say *no, thank you* if you don't want to do a thing?

Or *I am scared?*

How about *this seems dangerous?*

Is it babyish to say *no?*

Is it lying to say *yes, I want to* if NO you do NOT want to?

I had a lot of questions and no
answers, up at the top of those stairs.

Chapter
40

"I don't know how," I said.

"Fine, I'll show you," Cali said.

"Really?"

"Sure," she said.

Babyish Cali knelt down and put her pillow right on the edge of the top step.

She lowered her belly
onto the pillow.

She took a deep breath.

And then
she pushed off
with her feet and
sledded headfirst down
those stairs yelling,

WAHOOOEEEEEE—OH
ACK
URMFFFFF!

Chapter 41

Babyish Cali was a crumpled heap at the bottom of the stairs.

"Are you okay?" I asked from the top.

She turned around and there was blood all in her mouth.

"I'll get the moms!" I said.

I dropped my pillow up there and ran quickly but carefully down the stairs.

I ran past Babyish Cali.

But then I stopped and went back.

"I'll be right back," I said. "Hang in there, pal."

"Okay," Babyish Cali said.

I could tell she was trying not to cry.

"You're being very brave," I told her.

I patted her hair and ran to find the moms.

Chapter 42

"Sledding?" Mom asked.

Babyish Cali's mom was rushing inside.

Mom and I followed her.

As soon as Babyish Cali saw her mother, she started crying for real.

"What happened?" asked her

mom. "Let me see your mouth. What
happened?"

"I wanted to show Elizabeth I'm
not babyish," Babyish Cali was
saying.

"I don't understand," her mom
said.

"She calls me Babyish Cali and I
wanted . . ."

"Okay. Stop trying to talk, sweetheart. Oof, that's a lot of blood. Does it hurt?"

"Not really." She wouldn't look at me. "I just wanted to prove I'm not . . ."

"Shh," said her mom. "I think we have to go to the doctor and get this checked out."

"Of course," my mom said. "Do you want us to come, or . . ."

"No," the other mom said. "I think we better just go."

Mom grabbed me by the hand and pulled me toward their front door.

Chapter
43

Mom didn't put on the radio or even say *buckle up*.

I buckled anyway.

At a red light, Mom said, "Do you call her Babyish Cali?"

"Um," I said.

"The truth."

"Not no," I said.

"You call her Babyish Cali?!"

"It's a nickname," I said.

"It's a mean name," Mom said.
"Why would you do that?"

"I don't know," I said. "She is a
little babyish, I thought."

"And so you thought calling her

a nasty name would be okay?" Mom asked.

I shrugged. "Everybody calls her that."

"Really?" Mom asked. "Seems to me like somebody needs to be brave and say *hey, stop name-calling! That's rude*."

"I guess," I said. "Maybe I'm not as brave as you think I am."

"How would you feel if someone called you Babyish Elizabeth?"

That made me cry a little.

"They kind of do!" I yelled. "They aren't letting me in the Big Mouth Club!"

"So I guess you can imagine how Cali feels," Mom said.

"Except for the bleeding," I said.

Chapter
44

After bath and pajamas, I had to call
Babyish Cali. I didn't want to.

"It's too hard," I said.

"Sometimes the hard thing is the
right thing," Dad said.

Mom handed me the phone while it
was ringing.

I pretended to be Super Elizabeth, brave enough to do this.

I didn't believe it.

I was just plain Elizabeth, sad and scared.

A dad answered.

I said, "Hello this is Elizabeth who was over today when Cali got a bloody mouth may I please speak with Cali?"

The dad said, "Hold on."

"Hi!" Cali said.

I sat down under the table. "How are you?" I asked her.

"Fine," she said. "How are you?"

"Well, my mouth didn't get bloody."

She laughed. "True! My two front teeth are knocked out!"

"Lucky," I said. "Now you'll be in the Big Mouth Club."

"I didn't think about that."

"I did," I said sadly.

"Well . . ." she started, but I did not want to talk about that.

At all.

So I interrupted her to say the

thing Mom told me to say: "Sorry I called you babyish."

"Thanks," she said.

It sounded like *thankth*.

Just like how Bucky sounds.

I guess because of the lack of baby teeth up front.

I hung up and made a new wish:

I hope someday my *thankth* sounds so cute like that.

Chapter
45

Sunday morning, I threw away my page that just had the title

"The Night My Brother, Justin, Turned into a Hamster."

I started over and wrote a story called

"Elizabeth and the Missing Tooth."

In the story, a girl named Elizabeth is the first one in her whole class to lose a tooth.

Everybody thinks she is terrific and brave and grown-up.

It was a great story.

But it wasn't true.

The rest of Sunday, I pretended to be a dog.

Qwerty doesn't have to go to second grade and be left out of clubs.

Chapter
46

I had to go to
school anyway.

Chapter 47

At recess, nobody raced to the swings.

Everybody was too busy looking at Cali's new smile.

"I guess you can be in the Big Mouth Club now!" Anna told her. "Congratulations!"

"No, thankth," Cali said.

"What do you mean?" Anna asked.

"I don't want to be in the Big Mouth Club," Cali said. "I'm already in a club."

"What club?" Mallory asked her.

"With Elizabeth," Cali said.

Everybody looked at me.

It wasn't the truth.

I shrugged.

I didn't want to lie, but I did want to be in a club.

With Brave Cali.

"Yeah," I said. "We're friends."

"A club of just Cali and Elizabeth?" Anna asked.

"No, silly!" Cali said. (It came out, *No, thilly!*) "You can be in it, too! It's a club for everybody."

Chapter
48

"That's a dopey club," Smelly Dan said. "It's for dopey kids like Babyish Cali."

"No, it's not," I said. "And she's not babyish. So pipe down, you."

"Oh yeah?" Smelly Dan asked.

"Who wants to be in a club that lets everyone in?"

"I do," I said, standing right up to him.

I felt like Super Elizabeth, doing that.

"Me too," said Bucky, next to me.

"Can boys be in your club?"

"Of course!" Cali said.

"How about kids in Class 2A?" Rose asked.

"Yes," I said. "Absolutely. It's a club for everybody."

"Cool," Rose said.

Cali smiled. A big, toothless smile.

Chapter
49

I smiled back at her with all my baby
teeth showing.

Whatever.

I am in the club.

With everybody.

Nobody's left out.

We're all right in.

Even Dan.

I am trying to not call him Smelly Dan anymore.

Chapter
50

Not everything in life is easy.

Acknowledgments

With thanks and love to:

Amy Berkower, Elizabeth's champion

Elizabeth's best friends at Feiwel and Friends: Liz Szabla, Jean Feiwel, Liz Dresner, Kim Waymer, and Starr Baer

Paige Keiser, new partner and pal in Elizabeth's world

Zachary and Liam, with all their big teeth now, still friends with each other and me (even when it's not easy)

Nina, who checks to make sure I've cracked the truth of a little girl with gigantic feelings

My nieces, nephews, cousins, and kid friends who share their funny stories

Mitch, best guy to be around whether I'm up in the dumps or down in them

Mom and Dad, who have loved me through unlost and lost teeth, friends, roller skates, and schemes

The news, for being so unrelenting that my normally chill feelings feel fiercer, and the quest to inculcate empathy feels even more urgent than it's ever felt before

Carin, Meg, Deborah, Lynn, Stacy, Tracy, and more: my virtual club of writers

Mrs. Sudak, my second-grade teacher, who taught me to deal with disappointments like teeth that wouldn't fall out by making up stories and teaching me that you can make anything you imagine happen, if you are the writer

And all the other teachers like Mrs. Sudak, librarians like Katie Dersnah Mitchell, and parents like my own—who put pencils and books in their kids' hands, knowing those are the real magic wands

Thank you for reading this Feiwel and Friends book.

The Friends who made

possible are:

Jean Feiwel, Publisher

Liz Szabla, Associate Publisher

Rich Deas, Senior Creative Director

Holly West, Senior Editor

Anna Roberto, Senior Editor

Val Otarod, Associate Editor

Kat Brzozowski, Senior Editor

Alexei Esikoff, Senior Managing Editor

Kim Waymer, Senior Production Manager

Anna Poon, Assistant Editor

Emily Settle, Associate Editor

Starr Baer, Senior Production Editor

Liz Dresner, Associate Art Director

Follow us on Facebook or visit us online at mackids.com

Our books are friends for life.